Bruised Heart

J.M. GOODRICH

Bruised Heart

This book contains two short stories about finding love and happiness after having your heart broken. No matter how bad things may seem now, it will always get better.

About The Author

J.M. Goodrich is a native of Michigan's beautiful upper peninsula. She loves spending time outdoors as much as she can with her family when she's not reading or writing. She has been published in several different anthologies and novels of her own. She has written stories of romance, fantasy, and horror. In addition to her love of writing, she has a passion for music, and an obsession with The Beatles.

Also By J.M. Goodrich

Tiny Miracles

All her adult life, Beth has wanted children of her own. Now that she's finally married, she figures it's time. Only, there's one huge problem standing in her way - her new husband doesn't want kids. With the news of her best friend's pregnancy, Beth can't help but drown in jealousy, and is forced to enjoy this special time from a distance. She sticks by her best friend along her journey into motherhood, still hopeful that her husband will change his mind.

Will Beth's dream of becoming a mother ever come true?

One

BETH WOKE up in a much better mood that she normally did. A few weeks ago her best friend had called with the news that she was pregnant. She had been so excited for her friend that Beth practically jumped up and down for the rest of their conversation. She had always loved kids and couldn't wait to have one of her very own.

She quickly got dressed, grabbed the stack of books off her nightstand, and headed downstairs. Once in the kitchen she smiled brightly at Danny, her new husband. "Good morning!" She beamed, setting the books down on the table before giving her man a kiss. She had a good feeling about today.

He smiled back. "Morning. You seem like you're in a good mood," he chuckled. "Sleep well?"

"I did! Plus, I have something exciting to discuss with you," Beth said, motioning towards the stack of books on the table. Back when they had just gotten engaged was when Beth brought up the subject of children for the first time.

"Soon," her then husband-to-be had promised her, chuckling. "Let's worry about getting married first." To Beth, that had sounded like a solid promise. And one she wouldn't soon forget.

Danny set down the cup of coffee he was holding and started looking through the pile, reading all the titles. "Uh, Beth . . . these are all baby books . . ."

She clapped her hands together excitedly. "Uh, huh!"

He set the books back down and turned to look his wife in the eyes. "Please say this is all the info for Adrienne. She's the one that's pregnant, right?" he asked, glancing down quickly at his wife's stomach, which was still flat.

Beth let out a small laugh and moved to put her arms around her husband. "She is, yes. But I was hoping that we could . . . I don't know. Maybe talk about having one of our own. Soon." she said with a hopeful twinkle in her eye.

Danny, growing visibly uncomfortable, wiggled out of her grasp and took a step back. He ran his hands through his hair while he tried to figure out a way to tell his wife the truth. "Beth . . ." he started, his tone making her tense up a bit. He really didn't want to talk about this right now, but he supposed he was lucky to have avoided it for as long as he had. The fact that Beth had wanted children was no secret. Everyone knew that she did. And he was afraid to let her down. He loved her so much, and disappointing his wife was the last thing he wanted to do. But with Beth in his life, he felt like his life was finally complete. He didn't need or really want anything more. And that included children.

He took a deep breath and avoided looking his wife in the eyes as he spoke the words he was sure would break her heart. "I. . . I'm not sure I want kids."

She just stared at him, unblinking for what felt like an eternity. He nervously shifted from one foot to the other.

When she finally spoke her voice sounded so small, and cracked with emotion. "You mean, right now. Right? You're not sure if you want them now?"

"I mean, ever. Beth, I'm so sorry," he said quickly, before she could get in another word. "I really am, you have no idea."

"Just a year ago. . ." she said through the tears that streamed steadily down her face, "just a year ago when

I asked. . . you said you couldn't wait to start a family with me. I swore you seemed as excited as I felt when we discussed it back then." She turned away to blow her nose and mop up her face.

"I know, and back then I thought that's what I wanted," he began.

Beth whipped around to look her husband in the face. "Back then?" She practically yelled. "That was only a year ago. What could possibly have happened in just a year to change your mind about this?" She demanded. Danny stepped forward to try to put his arms around her, but she moved out of his reach, not wanting to be touched right now. The hurt look on his face almost made her feel bad. Almost. Instead, she cleared her throat. "Well? What happened?" She demanded again.

"What happened?" He repeated, anger seeping into his voice. "Nothing happened. I never really wanted children. Not now, not ever. I'll admit, I got caught up in all your excitement that day, but that was it. I'm sorry," he said again, his voice slowly softening. "I know I should have told you the truth from the beginning. I just didn't realize how big of a deal this was to you and . . ." he let out a sigh, "I didn't want to lose you, Beth."

4

"Didn't want to lose me?" she asked with a confused look across her face.

Danny plopped himself down on one of the kitchen chairs. "Yeah. I mean, with all the talk you did of having kids, would you still have wanted to marry me if you knew I didn't want them?"

Beth felt like she had been slapped across the face. She opened her mouth to respond but closed it again when she couldn't find the words to say.

"I didn't think so," Danny replied, letting out a shaky breath. Neither moved to comfort the other and they didn't speak to each other for the rest of the morning. That great feeling Beth felt waking up was long gone. Her heart felt like it was breaking into a million pieces.

Danny silently finished his breakfast and headed off to work, without giving Beth her usual kiss goodbye.

Two

"WOW, so he's lied to you this entire time?" Adrienne asked through the phone. As soon as Danny had left for work Beth went up to their bedroom, threw herself across the bed, and let herself cry it all out. She shed tears of grief for the child she might never get to hold and love, tears of anger and betrayal for her husband, and plain old tears of sadness, for her marriage would no longer be the same.

She continued to sniffle as she answered her friend. She thought she had shed every last tear she had, but she was wrong. "He has," she hiccuped. "I don't even know what to feel right now. I'm hurt, angry, confused . . . and it's all making my head hurt."

"Danny's at work all day, right?" Adrienne asked, knowing the answer. "So why don't you take a nice shower and get a nap. You'll feel loads better, I promise. Get yourself all cleaned up, rested up, and then we'll do something together. Non-baby-related if it'll make you feel better."

Beth laughed. "No, baby-related is fine. At least I'll get to experience it all through you," she laughed weakly, trying to sound brave but failing miserably. "We can do something now even, no need to wait until later," she offered.

Adrienne yawned loudly into the phone. "To tell you the truth, I could use a nap myself, it's kind of why I suggested it," she laughed. "You wouldn't believe how much energy it takes out of you just being pregnant," she laughed again. "So see you soon? In a few hours?"

"Deal," Beth said. She might never get to experience just how exhausting it truly is being pregnant, but she did know that a good cry will wear you out and make you plenty tired. She yawned herself as the thought of a nap became more and more appealing. But first, a shower.

"These are so cute!" Adrienne squealed as she held up a tiny dress with matching sparkly shoes. "I need these.

I need all of these," she said, gesturing to the rows of neatly hung baby dresses. Beth had to admit, they really *were* cute. She had always wanted a little girl of her own. At least, she thought to herself, I'd get to spoil Adrienne's little girl. And that's exactly what she planned on doing.

As much fun as she was having, Beth couldn't stop thinking about the heartbreaking conversation that took place in her kitchen just this morning. She was beginning to feel like she didn't know her husband at all anymore. She had thought they were on the same page baby-wise.

Adrienne noticed that her friend seemed a bit preoccupied. "Hey, are you okay?" She asked.

"Fine," Beth lied, "Just fine, promise." She offered a weak smile.

"Uh, huh," Adrienne said slowly, squinting to get a better look at her friend. "Somehow . . . I don't believe you." She stood there, arms crossed, until she broke Beth down.

"I'm sorry," she said, holding back more tears. "This has been an absolute roller coaster of a day, emotion-wise. And it's only half over." Adrienne remained silent, allowing Beth to get it all out. "I just can't believe Danny lied to me all this time." She turned to look at her friend. "I'm being crazy, aren't I?

I feel like I'm making this out to be a bigger deal than it really is. I'm sorry."

"You have absolutely nothing to be sorry for," Adrienne said as she picked up a pink onesie with matching fairy wings. "Having a child is a life changing decision. It's pretty serious, and what Danny did to you is not fair one bit. He flat out lied to you, hun. For years. Made you believe you wanted the same things, told you what he thought you wanted to hear, all so he wouldn't lose you. I know you love him Beth, but you have to admit, that was pretty selfish of him."

Beth knew she was right, he really was being selfish. None of this was okay. And she should be able to trust her husband. She shook her head, wanting to rid herself of all the negative thoughts. "You're right," she finally said," but can we please talk about something else? Like that?" She pointed to the tiny fairy outfit.

Adrienne held it up. "I know, right?" Isn't this just the cutest thing ever? I need it. I'm buying it."

"You have to save some things for the rest of us to buy for you," Beth laughed. She was already running out of ideas. It had only been about two or three months since Adrienne had found out she was pregnant, but boy did she love to shop. There'd be nothing left to get by the time her baby shower rolled around.

Three

BETH PULLED into her driveway and just sat in her parked car. She knew Danny would be home in a few minutes from work and she wasn't quite ready to face him just yet. Earlier Adrienne had suggested she take some time for herself, focus on the things she loves for a while and let things cool down between her and her husband. "You don't want to accidentally say something you'd later regret," she had said.

Putting the car in reverse she decided to take her friend's advice. She hadn't painted in forever, Beth never seemed to have the time anymore. It used to be her way of relaxing, of getting away from the disappointments and stress that life often seemed to bring.

Like today. So off she went for fresh painting supplies.

Arms loaded with bags of paint, brushes, and blank canvases, Beth began to make her way down to their basement. When she and Danny had first moved into this house she had meant to set up her own art studio in one of the spare rooms that they had down there. So far it contained an empty easel and a wooden stool for her to sit on. That was it. Although he hadn't come right out and said it directly, Beth always knew that he thought her art was nothing more than a waste of time. Sure, it was just a hobby for her and not a career, but she loved it nonetheless.

"What do you have there?" Danny asked, stopping her as she reached the top of the basement stairs.

Dang it, she thought. Almost made it. Beth slowly turned around to answer her husband. "Art supplies," she said, lifting the bags slightly. "I've decided I'm going to take up painting again."

"Well, could you maybe do it later? We should finish the conversation we started this morning, don't you think?" He didn't mean to come off as aggressive as he did. It just came out that way. He wasn't angry, but he felt like she was wasting her time painting. Besides, she was the one that brought up the issue at breakfast, not him.

"I don't think there's anything left to say. Not right now," Beth said with a shake of her head. "And anyway, you seemed dead set with your answer. Apparently you have been for years." She almost flinched at the hurt that flashed in his eyes. But she held her stance. Before anything else could be said she adjusted her supplies and quickly descended the stairs.

Setting down the bags, Beth closed the door behind her and let out a long breath. She had never fought with Danny before. She hated every second of it. She closed her eyes and wished she could turn back time to last night, when her life had seemed perfect.

Clearing her mind of anything baby-related, Beth locked the door, turned off her cell phone, and finally set up her art studio. She quickly got lost in the brush strokes, the colors, the possibilities of a blank canvas. Soon enough, she began to feel like her old self again.

After a few hours Beth wiped off her brush and stepped back to examine her work. At first she had painted only dark pictures, to match her mood. Then, she picked up the pinks and yellows and began working on some cheerful art that would hopefully hang in the bedroom of her best friend's baby girl. Even after the long break from painting, her art turned out pretty good, at least she thought so. Beth couldn't wait to bring the finished pieces to Adrienne's baby shower.

She jumped as a knock came at the door. Beth

opened it to see Danny standing there, with a sad look on his face. "I um, made dinner, if you're hungry. It'll be done in about five minutes."

"Thanks," she replied. Danny never made dinner, it had always been up to her to make it. She guessed it was his way of saying he was sorry. "I just have to clean up, then I'll join you."

Danny said nothing, but looked around the room with a slight look of disappointment.

Beth had caught it. So much for an apology, she thought. Danny headed back upstairs as she capped all her paints, making sure they were on tightly. She washed out her brushes and laid them out on a clean towel to dry. She took one more look at her work, feeling proud of herself. For the first time that day she smiled, truly smiled.

Dinner was. . . stressful. The chicken was black, the mashed potatoes were basically soup, and the green beans were ice cold. Beth pushed the food around her plate without actually trying any of it.

"I know it's not the best," Danny admitted. "I can't remember the last time I actually cooked anything." He gave the food a disgusted look. Beth just stared silently at her plate.

He cleared his throat. "Look, Beth. I really am sorry," he started. She didn't know how to answer him.

It certainly wasn't okay, and she wasn't sure it would be again. Danny went on. "I should have told you the truth from the beginning. I was so in love with you. I still am. That hasn't changed. Once I knew how much you wanted kids I figured the fact that I didn't would be a dealbreaker. And that I would lose you."

Anger was beginning to build in Beth. Keeping her eyes on the table she finally found her voice. "So, instead of telling me the truth and letting me decide what I wanted to do regarding our future, you chose to lie to me and take away my choice." It wasn't a question. She put her hands on the table. "You had no right to do that to me. If you truly loved me you would have just told me the truth," she challenged. "We could have figured something out together. Having children means a lot to me, yes. But it's not everything," she said, raising her head to look her husband in the eye. "*You* were everything to me. Everything else came after. It was always you. But now I feel like our entire life together has been one big lie." She stood up from the table, not wanting to talk about this anymore. And for once, she had the confidence to stand up for herself, and she didn't want to give Danny the chance to say something that would ruin it. "Now, if you'll excuse me, I'm going to go to bed. I'm not hungry, and it's been a trying day." As she walked away, Danny grabbed her wrist.

"Please," he pleaded. "Please talk to me. Don't run away. We can fix this. After all, it's really not that big a deal, let's not make it that way."

With that she yanked her arm from his grasp and stomped up to their bedroom, not turning around once to see his expression. She would not allow him to break her. She was nice enough though to leave his pillow and a couple blankets in the hall before locking the bedroom door.

Four

BETH WOKE up the next morning feeling worse than she had the night before. She had barely slept, her thoughts keeping her awake and in tears. In one day her marriage had gone from being absolutely perfect, at least in her mind, to one filled with lies and lacking trust. Her husband felt almost like a stranger to her now.

She laid in bed a lot longer than usual. She lacked the will and motivation to get up. Danny had knocked on the door some time ago, probably needing fresh clothes for work, but Beth hadn't cared. She simply rolled over and ignored him until he gave up and walked away. She knew she should probably feel a little bad about it, but she just didn't have it in her.

She would have stayed in bed all day if the phone

hadn't rang. Beth wouldn't have answered it, but it was blasting the bouncy song she had set for Adrienne's number.

"Hey girl, took you long enough to answer," she laughed. "How are you feeling today?"

Horrible, depressed, like my heart has been ripped out and stomped on, she wanted to say. But she didn't want her friend to worry any more than she already was, so she just answered, "Fine. I'm just tired." She yawned.

But her friend knew her better than that. "Listen, I have some running around to do today-some errands, shopping, and a doctor's appointment. Hubs is busy with work, so what do you say to coming with me?" She asked brightly.

Beth scrunched up her face. "To your appointment?" She asked. That didn't sound like much fun to her.

"Yeah, silly, to my appointment. It's just an ultrasound today, so you'll get to see the little nugget. Little nugget was what she was calling her baby for now since they hadn't settled on a name yet. "I thought maybe it might cheer you up a bit."

Beth found herself laughing. It would be kind of cool to see the ultrasound. She hadn't seen one in real life before, just in the movies. Keeping busy would help take her mind off of things anyway. "Sure," she told her friend. "I'd love to go with you. How long do I have before I have to be ready?"

"About an hour? I'll swing by and pick you up."

"Sounds great, see you in a bit." Beth hung up the phone and tolled out of bed. She really wasn't planning on doing anything today, but it also wasn't like her to just sit, or lie, at home all day. So she got dressed, grabbed her purse, and waited outside on the porch until she spotted Adrienne's car coming down the street.

"Well, you're looking better than you sounded on the phone."

Beth stood up and dusted herself off. "Clean clothes and fresh air will do that to you," she replied as she hopped in the car. "So, where to first?"

Adrienne put the car in reverse. "First off is the doctor's," she squealed. "This is only my second ultrasound, so the baby will be very tiny, but it's still so exciting!"

Beth smiled at her friend's excitement. Hopefully, she thought, some of it would rub off onto me. Beth's smile faltered knowing this might be the only way she'd get to experience something like this. It wouldn't be her baby's image on the screen, she wouldn't get to feel its little kicks and flutters. Beth stared out the window, hoping Adrienne hadn't noticed the shift in her mood.

The appointment went even better than she thought it would. Seeing the image of the little bean, as the ultrasound technician called it, made Beth feel so happy. Even though she'd never get to do this herself, Beth felt excited for her friend. Being by her side during her whole pregnancy would help Beth fulfill at least a little of her desire for motherhood. She'd take what she could get.

Next was lunch, and while they were in the middle of eating Danny tried to call, but Beth kept pressing the 'ignore' button. She had nothing to say to him right now. Adrienne noticed but didn't say anything. She knew that once her friend was ready to open up she would. Beth finally switched her phone off and threw it in the bottom of her purse.

"So have you given any thought to an idea for your baby shower?" She asked as she stabbed a pile of lettuce.

"Oh, my gosh. I have so many ideas. I need you to help narrow them down," Adrienne replied as she retrieved a list from her purse.

Reading down the list, Beth found the perfect one. "This is it," she pointed.

"Fairies! I love it! I love them all, but that's why I needed you," she laughed.

"Also, it goes with that little outfit we saw in the store the other day," Beth pointed out.

"You mean the one I bought," Adrienne laughed even harder. "I couldn't help myself. It was the cutest thing I had ever seen and I just couldn't resist."

Beth nodded in agreement. "We could even display the outfit somehow, and center the theme and decorations around it," she suggested.

Adrienne's eyes grew wide with excitement. "That is absolutely perfect. We have some serious shopping to do," she said. "After our salads, of course."

Beth already started making a mental list of everything they'd need. She couldn't wait to help put together the perfect fairy-themed baby shower. Plus, the paintings she had secretly done for Adrienne would make perfect additions to the decor.

Five

ADRIENNE'S BABY shower was a few months later, closer to her due date. The closer it got, the more excited she and Beth had become. Between the stress of making her best friend's baby shower absolutely perfect and the stress of everything going on at home, Beth had come down with a bug.

"It's just a cold, I'm fine," she reassured Adrienne the night before the party. "I haven't been sleeping much with everything going on with me and Danny. I worry about every little thing."

She still wasn't entirely sure what she wanted to do about her marriage. On one hand, she loved Danny with everything she had. She'd been in love with him for years. They had been friends first, when they met way back at college. Things seemed much simpler then, back when Beth had thought they shared the same hopes and dreams for their future. That seemed like a lifetime ago now. But, if she stayed with him, she'd be giving up her dream of motherhood. As much as she tried these past few months, she just couldn't get her husband to change his mind. He kept telling her he loved her, wanted to be with her still, and that his job was just too important right now. There's no time for a baby, he'd argue. And she'd feel betrayed all over again. Beth spent many nights alone, crying over the loss of her dreams and the betrayal of the man she loved.

Danny had been trying to win her over, by learning to cook, cleaning the house every day top to bottom, buying her little gifts. Although they made her smile and showed that he cared for her, he could never give her what she really, truly wanted.

"You go sit down," Beth told her very pregnant friend. "I got this," she motioned to the pile of decorations that still needed to be put up, and the balloons that needed helium. "Go put your feet up and rest. I'll even let you yell at me if I hang something up in the wrong place," she winked.

"Deal!" Adrienne said, grabbing a handful of carrot sticks before taking a seat.

The entire place was a sea of pink and sparkles. Fairies were everywhere-taped to the walls, hung from the ceiling, little figurines played in the centerpieces on the tables. Even the balloons were shaped like fairies.

Danny would have hated this, Beth thought to herself with a smile. She started to get a little light-headed from moving up and down chairs and step ladders all day so she decided that she had earned a break as well.

"What do you think?" She asked as she plopped down next to Adrienne. All that was really left was to hang up the paper lanterns. They could wait a few minutes.

Adrienne looked around the room with a huge smile on her face. "It looks absolutely magical," she replied. "I wish I could have a party like this everyday." That made them both laugh.

At the same moment both Adrienne's and Beth's husbands walked through the door. Beth jerked her head towards her best friend.

Adrienne shrugged. "I thought you'd want him here," she said innocently. Beth shook her head in disbelief. She never would have thought Danny would ever have stepped foot in a place like this. And she didn't even think to invite him herself.

"It's very. . . pink in here," Adrienne's husband said, kissing her on the cheek and handing her a small bag. "Hi beautiful."

"Hi." She beamed at him.

"Well, you are having a girl," Beth pointed out. "And we wanted everything to match the fairy outfit we bought."

He raised an eyebrow. "For you or the baby?" he laughed.

"I never showed you, did I?" Adrienne giggled. "I was so excited about it that I had put it right in the baby's closet so it wouldn't get lost or ruined." She brought him over to show him the outfit, which we had hung directly over the cake so everyone would be able to see it. Beth almost wished that they had thought to buy some fairy wings for themselves now.

Beth and Danny just stood by each other, awkward and silent for a bit while Adrienne gushed over the decorations and everything.

"Did you do all this?" Danny asked, clearing his throat.

"I did," Beth said, kicking invisible dirt around.

"Well, it looks great," he offered. Beth just smiled.

Adrienne called out from the opposite side of the room. "Hey Beth! Can I borrow you for a minute? Important girl stuff!" She winked. At least, Beth thought it was a wink. She was too far away to tell for certain.

Beth rolled her eyes while laughing. "Be right back," she told Danny.

Adrienne quickly ushered her friend to the ladies room. "I don't have to hold your dress or anything while you pee, do I?" she laughed. "I thought that only applied to wedding dresses."

"Ha. Ha. And it does. But here," she handed Beth the bag her husband had brought with him. "This is for you."

Beth opened up the bag. "You can't be serious," she said as she pulled out a pregnancy test.

Adrienne folded her arms across her chest. "I can, and I am. Beth, you've been feeling sick lately"'

"Stress," Beth pointed out.

"Well, yes. I'm sure stress plays a part in it. But it hasn't gone away. Plus," she sucked in air between her teeth, "you've put on a little weight, hun."

"No, I didn't," Beth cried, rushing to the mirror. "Okay, maybe a little. But just a little." She noticed just now that her face did look a bit puffy.

She turned back to face her friend. "But Danny

and I only . . . you know . . . once in the past few months. He had been overly romantic trying to win me back. We got caught up in the moment." She smiled briefly at the memory before shaking her head.

"And what about birth control?" Adrienne asked her.

Beth's face turned bright red. "I kinda stopped once Danny and I stopped talking," she admitted.

"Well, all right. Get your ass in there and take the test," she turned Beth around and pointed in the direction of the stalls.

Three minutes can be an awfully long time, as Beth is now finding out. After she checked her watch, she picked up the test, and her heart stopped. Stepping out of the stall, tears streaming down her face, she handed the test over to her impatient best friend, who immediately started screaming and jumping up and down.

After a few minutes she steered a still-stunned Beth out of the bathroom and towards her husband.

"Beth, what's wrong?" he asked, concern etched all over his face. Wordlessly, she handed him the test, afraid of what his response was going to be. He took one look at it and his eyes grew so wide Beth was sure they were going to pop right out of his head.

"Is this. . . Beth, is this yours?" He turned to Adrienne. "You didn't do this, right? As a joke?"

Adrienne shook her head. "Nope, that's all her. And you, I guess." She added with a wink.

"So we're . . ."

"Going to have a baby," Beth finished for him. She stared at her husband and was shocked when a smile crept across his face.

"Really? I'm . . .I'm going to be a father?"

"Looks that way."

Before she could say anything else he swept her up in a hug and showered her with kisses. "Oh, Beth. I'm so, so sorry," he said into her hair.

"For what?"

"Well," he said, looking down at the test again. "I never knew, until this moment, how much I really did want to become a father."

Beth grinned. "So this is a good thing?" She asked.

"The best!" he yelled. He bent down to kiss her belly. "Hello, my tiny miracle."

"Double baby shower!" Adrienne laughed, enveloping both of them in a giant hug.

Beth put her hand on her stomach. Tiny miracle, indeed, she thought to herself as she began to cry again. This time they were tears of happiness.

Room For Two More

J.M. Goodrich

Room For Two More

Katie's father has always been extra protective of her. Her mother had taken off as soon as she had given birth, wanting nothing to do with either of them. Not that he would ever let Katie know. Joe tried his hardest to shield his little girl from any and all pain and heartache. He spent so much time and energy on her that he neglected his own feelings. Until one day he meets a single mom with a daughter Katie's age. As the kids grew closer, so did their parents. Still guarding his heart, Joe is unsure of what to do with his feelings.

Will he stay closed off to love forever? Or does his heart have room for two more?

One

KATIE SEARCHED the sea of faces in the auditorium. Her little face lit up from where she was peeking out from behind the curtain when she spotted her father. She knew he would be there, he always was. But that didn't stop her from getting excited at the sight of his face.

Joe absolutely adored his little girl. She was all he had left in this world, and he was fiercely protective of her. Since the very beginning it had been just the two of them. He refused to allow his sweet little girl to feel even a fraction of the pain and heartache that he had. But by doing everything that he can to make his daughter happy, Joe often forgets about himself.

Well, maybe not forget. More like he doesn't feel he's ready to let himself be open to another person again. So he hides his heart behind many thick walls. That little girl beaming at him from up on that dance stage is all that matters to him. And he wouldn't have it any other way.

Joe's heart filled with pride as he watched Katie dance. She had shown interest in it and loved dancing for as long as he can remember. It took a few months of her begging and batting her puppy dog eyes for him to break down and let her join a dance class. He was glad though that he did. He had never seen Katie happier than when she donned her ballet shoes and took to the stage.

"How was I, daddy?" Katie asked as she twirled towards her father. He bent down and scooped her up in his arms, planting a kiss softly on her cheek. "You were great, as always," he said, smiling proudly. "You might just be the best dancer I've ever seen."

"I am," Katie answered matter-of-factly, making Joe laugh. She sounded so serious. Joe gave her one more quick squeeze before setting her back down. "Can I go play with my friend Gabby?" she asked, looking around the room.

Joe put his hands on his hips and pretended to

look sad. "You mean you don't want to hang out with me?"

"Daddy!" Katie laughed as she shook her head, her ponytail swinging back and forth. "You're too old. I want to play with my friends."

"I'm old?" Joe asked his daughter, eyebrows raised.

Katie rolled her eyes. "Duh, daddy. You're a daddy, and that means you're old."

Joe shook his head. "Fair point. Well, then," he laughed. "Come on, let's go find Gabby. Since I'm too old."

Katie dashed off in search of her friend. Joe tried to keep an eye on her but it was difficult in the sea of tulle. All the young dancers looked similar to him with their matching outfits and hair all done up the same way.

He finally found them huddled together at the edge of the room, giggling away. Joe smiled to himself, he loved seeing his little girl so happy. It was what he lived for.

"There you are!" A woman's voice said, startling Joe. He turned to see one of the most beautiful women he had ever seen standing next to him. She had long, flowing chestnut hair, dark blue eyes, smooth skin. Feeling his cheeks turning red, Joe shook his head slightly and quickly looked away.

I shouldn't be thinking things like that, he thought to himself. I have no time for women in my life right now.

Ever since Katie's mother had left Joe tried his hardest to stay away from women, even just as friends. He wasn't ready to let himself be vulnerable again, and was beginning to think he never would be. So he turned all of his attention to his sweet Katie and made her his main focus. Everything else was either forgotten or pushed aside in his life. Including caring for himself.

The little girl just smiled up at her mother. "Can I play with Katie, mommy? Please?" She asked, batting her eyelashes.

"I'm guessing you're Katie?" She asked with a smile, looking at the girl standing next to her daughter. Katie nodded. She then turned to Joe and extended her hand. "You must be her dad. Hi, I'm Angie."

Joe hesitantly shook her hand. "Joe," was all he said. Clearing his throat he then added, "And yes, "I'm Katie's father." He withdrew his hand and stuck it in his pocket, staring awkwardly at the floor.

Angie knelt down in front of her daughter. "It's alright with me, as long as Katie's dad says it's okay," she said, smiling brightly at the girls. Angie stood back up. "What do you say, dad?" She asked Joe. He raised his eyebrows at her. Clearing her throat she added in a more serious tone, "Joe. I meant Joe."

"Well . . ."

"Please daddy? Please?" Katie pleaded before he could get out some type of excuse. He always had a few ready in case of situations like this. He hadn't been the most social person these past few years. Not wanting to disappoint his daughter, Joe reluctantly agreed.

"Yay! Thank you daddy!" Katie squealed as she jumped to hug her father. Turning to her friend she told her, "You can come play at my house. I have lots of toys."

Joe laughed nervously. "I guess we're all heading to my house then."

"Great. We'll follow you in our car," Angie replied.

So they loaded their girls into their separate vehicles and headed off to Joe's for their first playdate.

Two

"WOW!" Gabby yelled as she climbed out of her mother's car. Joe had filled his backyard with all sorts of playsets and toys for Katie to keep her occupied.

There was a mini picnic table where they enjoyed a lot of lunches and dinners, when the weather was nice enough. Next to that was a playhouse that Joe had built with his own two hands. It was made of wood with real working windows, doors, and lights. It looked exactly like a miniature version of their real house. Katie loved it. A sandbox, swing set with a slide, and various other outdoor toys littered the yard. There was plenty to keep the two girls busy for a while.

Joe smiled to himself as his two guests took it all in. "Impressive," Angie said. "We just have a swing set in our backyard, but it's only about half the size of yours.

"I do spoil her, that's for sure," Joe laughed, rubbing his hand across the back of his neck. "I just want my little girl to be happy. I guess I do overdo it sometimes. I can't help it."

"Nah," Angie replied. "Playtime and exercise are important for a child.

Gaby tugged on her mother's shirt. "Can I go play now?" She asked with wide, pleading eyes. Angie looked to Joe.

"Of course," he said, and the two girls ran screaming and laughing into the backyard.

Joe led Angie to the firepit in the corner of the yard. He had set up a couple chairs so he could sit by the fire and still keep a watchful eye on Katie as she played.

"This is a really nice setup," Angie said as she sank down into one of the chairs. "If this was my yard I'd probably spend more time out here than in the house."

"I think we do," Joe chuckled. He nodded towards his daughter. "I don't know where she gets all her energy from. Between all this and the dancing I can't keep up with her."

"It's a shame dance season is over now," Angie replied. "Gabby loves it more than anything. She's constantly dancing around the house."

"Katie too. Her entire room is decorated in ballerina pictures and ballet shoes. And pink. So. Much. Pink." He shook his head in amusement. He wondered briefly if he was sharing too much.

Angie looked him in the eyes and smiled sweetly. "Well, you sound like an amazing father. You have a happy, healthy little girl."

That statement made him blush, and he looked away. He didn't know what to say to that. Instead he watched as the girls slid down the slide a few times and then ran, laughing into the playhouse. "No old people allowed!" Katie yelled as she closed the door behind them. He could hear them giggling inside.

"So now I'm old?" Angie laughed, looking over to Joe with her mouth wide open.

Joe grinned. "Don't feel too bad, this is the second time today she's called me old. Right after the recital Katie told me I was too old to hang out with."

"Kids," Angie replied with a shake of her head. "They always say exactly what's on their mind."

"You get in trouble for that as an adult," Joe pointed out.

"I know. It's so not fair."

The girls continued exploring the yard, playing and giggling together. Even after having performed in the dance recital, they didn't seem to tire at all. They were two little balls of energy, darting around the yard.

After a few minutes of silence, with the exception of giggles and playful screams from the girls, Angie turned to Joe. "So," she took in a big breath, "is Katie's mom around?"

Joe just looked down at the ground. He opened his mouth to speak but changed his mind.

"I'm sorry," she said. "I didn't mean to bring up any feelings or anything . . ."

Joe shook his head. "No, it's nothing like that. Just . . .no one really asks about her, is all. And it's not exactly my favorite subject, I guess. She's, let's just say she's not involved. In any way," he replied in a tone that politely said he was finished with the topic.

"I'm sorry," Angie said in a low voice. She knew all too well that an absent parent can be a sore subject. "Same with Gabby's dad. She asks about him all the time," she shook her head sadly. "I never know what to say to her. I don't want to lie to her. But I know the truth would just break her heart. She's far too young for that. And again, I'm sorry. I won't bring it up again, promise," she held her hands up in surrender.

He knew just what she meant. He devoted his life to protecting his little girl from harsh truths and heartache. "It's alright," he assured her. "Just an uncomfortable subject, that's all."

"I totally agree with you there." Angie checked her

watch. "It's getting close to dinner time. I should take Gabby home soon. Or try to," she laughed as she watched the girls pushing plastic baby strollers around. "She seems to be having a lot of fun."

Joe looked at his own daughter, his face lighting up at how happy she was. It also made him feel a little guilty. Had he been keeping her from making friends, he wondered. He hated socializing himself, and tried to avoid it at all costs. But was it hurting his little girl? He had never realized it or even given it any thought before just now. He suddenly felt incredibly selfish. Clearing his throat he turned to Angie. "Well, maybe we can do this again," he suggested. "Gabby can come over here again or we can maybe take the girls to a park or something."

"Oh, Gabby would love that, thank you!" Angie replied happily. "They do seem to be getting along very well, don't they?" They turned their attention back to the girls, who were now burying each other in the sandbox.

"Gabby! Come on, honey!" Angie called. She watched as Gabby wiggled out of a pile of sand. It fell off her in waves as she made her way to her mom. That was sure to make a nice mess in the car.

"What, mom?"

Angie bent down to brush off some sand that was

stuck to her grubby little face. "It's starting to get late, hun. We gotta get home for dinner. And you need to wash up," she laughed.

"Aw mom, do we really have to?'

Katie chimed in, "Yeah, do they have to, daddy?"

"Afraid so, Katie. We have to get washed up and everything too. And I have some work to finish up."

"Okay." Katie replied sadly, staring down at her sandy little feet.

"But we will do this again, I promise," he assured his little girl. Her face lit up.

"Thanks daddy!"

The girls said their goodbyes and hugged each other. There were no hugs exchanged between the adults, but phone numbers and promises of getting the girls together soon were. Katie waved until Gaby's car was out of sight, then twirled and jumped into the house, leaving a trail of sand for her dad to sweep up.

Three

JOE HAD BEEN GOING BACK and forth all night, barely sleeping for the thoughts keeping him awake. On one hand, he wanted his daughter to be happy, and being with Gabby seemed to make her happy. Having friends, especially at this age, was important, he knew that. He felt so selfish for keeping her all to himself. She had never once complained though, so he had always just assumed that she was a happy, content little girl.

On the other hand, was he ready to be opened up to being hurt again? It was easier to continue being selfish, but was it really the best thing for the two of them? He hated being so conflicted. Up until just a few nights ago, everything was fine. Life was good, he was happy and focused only on his daughter-the light of his life. Now everything seemed messy and confusing. And he hated it.

Angie had called a couple times trying to arrange a second playdate for the girls. Joe had answered the phone each time, giving off some excuse as to why they couldn't meet up.

"Daddy? Can we go see Gabby today?" Katie asked as she wandered into the kitchen for breakfast. She was dressed in ballet flats and a tutu over top of her pj's. She rubbed the sleep out of her little eyes and looked up at her father.

He scooped her up in his arms. "Morning, sleepyhead."

She replied, "I'm hungry. And I miss my friend, daddy. Can we play together today? I'll be good."

Joe sighed heavily. He hated making his daughter upset. He supposed it was time to suck it up and let them play together. "Alright," he said, setting her down at the table. He walked over to retrieve her breakfast plate. It was bacon, eggs, and hashbrowns today. "I'll give them a call. But you have to finish your breakfast first."

"Okay, daddy."

As the two of them ate Katie told him all her plans for when she saw Gabby. It was shaping up to be a busy day, if she had her way.

Katie was excited to finally be able to see her friend again, so she ate her food in record time. After the plates were washed and the kitchen put back in order, Joe figured he might as well get this phone call over with.

Angie answered on the second ring. "Well, hello stranger,' she laughed into the receiver.

"Hi," he replied. He decided to just launch right into it, feeling very nervous all of a sudden. "Look, I know I've been kind of avoiding you. And that's not right."

"Uh huh. . . " Angie replied cautiously. She didn't want to say too much yet, for fear of scaring him off again.

Joe continued. "Gabby's a great girl. And she gets along so well with my Katie. She hasn't stopped asking about her since the recital. It's. . . well, it's you."

"Me?" she asked, a little shocked. "What on earth could I possibly have done?'

He sighed heavily again. "You haven't done anything. Really, it's me. I . . .it's a long story, but I don't exactly open myself up to people a lot. I got kind of . . . afraid, I guess. And you scared me."

"I . . . scared you?" Angie asked, amusement creeping into her tone. "I never meant to, I'm sorry."

"I know, it's something that I gotta work on. And

I'm trying. Or, I want to try. It's complicated," he said with a small laugh. "And since I'm trying to try, what do you think about possibly getting the girls together today?"

"I think it's a great idea, actually. Gabby has talked nonstop about Katie as well." She paused for a few seconds. "There's this park not far from my house. What do you say we meet there? They even have an ice cream stand. We could meet up after lunch, get some ice cream, and then the girls could run off and play."

"Sounds like a great idea to me."

"Awesome. I'll text you the address and everything. See you in a bit."

"Bye." As Joe hung up the phone he felt two little eyes on him.

"Are we going, daddy?" Katie asked, eyes wide with hope.

"We are. After lunch we're meeting them at a park. They have ice cream there," he added.

"I love ice cream!" Katie jumped up and down.

Joe laughed. "I know you do."

Katie raced off to her room. "I'm going to pick out some toys for the park!"

As Joe pulled his car into the parking lot he quickly spotted Gabby with her mom. It wasn't hard to see the girl in the hot pink jumping up and down with excitement. The second the car was put into park Katie had her seat belt unbuckled and was opening the door.

"Careful!" He yelled after her as she took off towards her friend.

"You made it!" Angie teased as he walked up to them.

He winked, "Couldn't resist getting some ice cream."

"Ice cream!" The girls yelled in unison.

Angie giggled. "Guess it's ice cream time."

The small group walked over to the ice cream stand, then found a bench to sit while they enjoyed their treats. Before too long both girls had sticky ice cream all over their faces.

"Can we go play now?" They asked, having finished already.

"Just as soon as I get you cleaned up a bit," Angie laughed as she pulled a couple wipes out of her purse.

As the now clean girls raced off towards the monkey bars, Angie turned to Joe. "We don't have to talk, if I make you uncomfortable," she told him. "I'm sure that I did. I honestly never meant to."

"No, it's . . . it's okay. Maybe talking can be part of

my whole 'trying to work on things,' he offered her a weak smile. He crossed his arms and slumped down a little, trying to get comfortable on the hard plastic bench.

"Gabby's dad has been gone about two years now," Angie said after a few minutes of silence. She figured she'd get the ball rolling, and that maybe talking about her own issues and whatnot would help Joe to open up, even just a little. She could tell that he was troubled by something. They had talked briefly during the many dance rehearsals throughout the year but had never formally introduced themselves to one another. Angie had thought that he was attractive and even had a little crush on him since the beginning of the year. But that was her little secret.

"I'm sorry," Joe replied.

Angie just shook her head. "Honestly, I'm glad. He was never good to me, and didn't really pay too much attention to Gabby at all. He sure pays attention to his other kids though," she scoffed. "He was never faithful to me, our entire relationship. I knew about it, I just tried hard to ignore it, to keep our family together. It was an incredibly stupid thing to do, I know," she said, wiping away a tear. Joe sat straight up, unsure of what to say.

"I'm sorry," was all that he could think of.

"It's my fault, you know. I should have left the second I found out. It took the news of his other children for me to actually gather the courage to leave him. His oldest . . .is the same age as Gabby."

"Wow," Joe replied. "That's awful. I'm so sorry you had to go through that. What about Gabby? What does she think about all this?"

Angie wiped her nose on a tissue she fished out of her purse. "She actually doesn't know. About the other kids. Her half-siblings, I guess." She shook her head again. "Once I left he didn't make any attempt to see or even talk to Gabby. Too busy with his other family, I suppose." She looked down at the ground, fearing she'd shared way too much.

"You probably think I'm an awful person now, don't you?" she asked in a timid voice.

"Absolutely not," Joe replied. "You went through a truly terrible situation. You did what you thought was best at the time, and put your daughter first. I call that strong." He tentatively scooted closer to Angie and put his arm lightly around her shoulder.

Angie sniffled. "Thanks. I didn't mean to get all super emotional on you."

"Hey, it's okay," he said softly. "It's an emotional issue."

She wiped her face dry and took in a deep breath. "It feels good to get it all out sometimes, though."

Joe took the hint. "I'm guessing that's my cue to unload," he said through a small laugh. "I apologize in advance if I become too emotional," he teased.

Before he began he looked to his daughter, happily playing with her new best friend.

"For her entire life, it's just been me and Katie," he said, shifting in his seat. "Her mother never wanted kids. She completely freaked out when the test came back positive-blaming me for trying to trap her in the relationship with the pregnancy and all that. Said I planned it," he shook his head sadly.

"I didn't plan it. I love Katie with all my heart. That little girl is everything to me. A small part of me had always hoped that once my ex gave birth and held her little girl in her arms that thing would change. That we'd be a happy little family. I was wrong. Very wrong."

"She resented me and berated me the entire nine months of her pregnancy. And then, as soon as she gave birth to Katie, she was gone. Like, that night she somehow slipped out of the hospital, leaving baby Katie there all alone. The hospital immediately called me, letting me know the situation. I wasn't allowed at the actual birth, the ex didn't want me there." Joe took in a deep, shaky breath.

"So I showed up at the hospital. It was love at first sight for me," he smiled at his little girl. "And since then I basically shut down my heart to anything and everyone but her," he nodded across the playground. "It's been tough, and I try so hard to protect her from anything bad happening. I know I can't protect her from everything, but a guy can try, right?" he managed a laugh.

"So that," he looked at Angie, "is basically making every excuse not to see you. I like you, I like being around you. And that scared me. And I'm sorry," he said softly as he hung his head.

It was Angie's turn to comfort him. "We all do crazy things when it comes to our kids sometimes," she said. "But it doesn't mean that we have to shut down emotionally. But thank you, for opening up to me. I know that wasn't easy."

"Oh, it wasn't," he admitted.

"It's the first step to healing though. And if you'll let me, I'd like to be there to help you."

"I think I'd like that," he said. And he meant it.

Four

JOE DID START to feel better emotionally after having confessed everything to Angie. He had never told anyone the real story before, it was just too painful for him. It still hurt to talk about, but he found small comfort in the fact that Angie went through a similar experience with Gabby's father.

Over the next few weeks they continued to get the girls together, almost daily. Joe had never seen Katie happier. He still couldn't believe how selfish he had been all those years. And hated the face that he was blind to it.

But with Angie's help he was slowly getting over it. And as the kids grew closer, so did their parents. There had been a date or two in between all the playdates, but nothing serious yet. Joe was happy to be taking things slow though.

They decided to end the summer with a weeklong camping trip. They had grown steadily closer over the course of the past few months and Joe decided he was finally ready to try something like this. Besides, they wouldn't be far out of town in case he did change his mind.

The weather had been absolutely perfect all week. Today was the last day of their trip. Next week the girls would start school and dance classes would be running again.

"You know, I'm proud of you, Joe. You've come a long way." Angie said as they walked along the beach. The girls were splashing around in the shallow water.

He looked at her with a raised eyebrow. "I have?"

"Yes,' she giggled. "For starters, you made it the entire week with me and Gabby. I kind of had doubts you would. Don't hate me," she laughed harder.

"I could never hate you, besides, I had doubted myself a bit at first," he admitted. "But being here on this trip with you was easier than I thought it would be."

"Oh, cuz I'm so difficult," she teased.

"Well, yes," he teased back, which earned him a light punch to the arm. "No, I've actually really enjoyed this week. Everything about it. And I'm a little sad it's ending so soon," he said as he took her hand in his.

Angie smiled brightly. "I am too. I think this camping trip was just what we all needed. I mean, look at those two," she nodded towards Gabby and Katie. They were now digging a giant hole in the sand and taking turns jumping in as it filled in with water.

"They have become pretty inseparable, haven't they?" he laughed.

"They're the best of friends. I wonder if they'll be in the same class at school. They are the same age, after all," she pointed out."

"That would be nice," Joe admitted, "but if not, they'll always have dance class."

"True."

"Plus," Joe said, stopping directly in front of Angie, "I have a feeling we'll still be seeing a lot of each other." He then leaned in and kissed Angie lightly on the lips. As he started to pull away she wrapped her arms around him and kissed him harder.

"Wow," she said.

"Not bad for a first kiss," Joe chuckled. "I have been wanting to do that all week."

"Well, you should have," Angie said breathlessly.

"Gross!" giggled Katie. "You kissed my daddy!"

Angie laughed and took a step back. "I sure did," she winked at Joe. "I hope that it was okay that I did that," she said to Katie.

"Um," Katie put her hand to her chin, pretending to think, "I guess so."

"Good, because I like him. I like you, too," Angie said, wiping sand off of Katie's nose.

"I like chocolate. And you're okay," she added.

"I'll take it."

Joe laughed as well. "And I take it the mention of chocolate means that it's bonfire and s'mores time?" he asked. It had started to get a little dark on them. They just hadn't noticed.

They gathered everything they had brought down to the beach with them and carried it back to their campsite. While the girls changed into dry clothes Angie gathered all the fixings needed for s'mores and Joe lit a nice fire.

Everyone sat around the roaring fire, toasting their marshmallows and warming up. The weather during the day was absolutely perfect, while the night tended to get a little chilly.

"Are you girls excited for school to start?" Angie asked them.

They both shook their little heads. "No," Katie answered. "I'm excited to dance again. I miss it."

"Me too," Gabby said, her mouth full of gooey marshmallow. "It's my favorite thing in the whole world."

"Daddy? Can I not do school this year? I just want to dance." Katie asked in a serious tone.

Joe put his arm lovingly around his daughter. "I know you do honey, but school is important, too."

"But why?" She pouted. "I don't want to do anything but dance, daddy."

"You have to go to school to learn things. Everyone does. It's just a part of life. I had to go to school when I was little. And I actually enjoyed it. Learning can be fun, if you let it."

"Me, too," added Angie.

"Yeah, a million billion years ago," Gabby giggled as she looked into the fire. She loved watching the flames dance around.

"Just how old do you think I am, young lady?" Angie laughed.

"I don't know." Gabby shrugged, "just really old."

"Ha, ha. Thanks kid." There was laughter all around the campfire that night.

For the first time since Katie was born, Joe began to feel that maybe, just maybe, he could have the family he's always wanted. One day. He was in no rush at the moment though. He was loving the way things were progressing with Angie. Everything about it just felt right. He was slowly beginning to feel that he might be worthy of love too. And that opening up his heart again maybe wasn't such a bad idea after all. He discovered that in his heart, he had room for two more.

www.ingramcontent.com/pod-product-compliance
Lightning Source LLC
Chambersburg PA
CBHW020340130626
46549CB00003B/1226